I0692454

Granville H. Meixell

John J. Ingalls

his life, his public services, and his personal characteristics - A biographical

sketch

Granville H. Meixell

John J. Ingalls
his life, his public services, and his personal characteristics - A biographical sketch

ISBN/EAN: 9783337388720

Printed in Europe, USA, Canada, Australia, Japan

Cover: Foto ©Andreas Hilbeck / pixelio.de

More available books at **www.hansebooks.com**

JOHN J. INGALLS

HIS LIFE, HIS PUBLIC SERVICES, AND HIS

PERSONAL CHARACTERISTICS

A BIOGRAPHICAL SKETCH

BY

GRANVILLE H. MEIXELL
M.A. (VANDERBILT)

PROFESSOR OF THE ENGLISH LANGUAGE AND
LITERATURE, HISTORY, ECONOMICS,
AND SOCIAL SCIENCE IN
MIDLAND COLLEGE

PRESS OF
THE HOME PRINTING COMPANY
ATCHISON, KANSAS
1896

TO

MRS. JOHN J. INGALLS

IN

GRATEFUL REMEMBRANCE

OF THE

KIND AND GENEROUS SERVICE RENDERED

TO THE AUTHOR IN ITS PREPARATION,

THIS BIOGRAPHICAL SKETCH

IS MOST RESPECTFULLY

DEDICATED

PREFATORY NOTE

This essay appeared in substantially the same form in the issues of THE MIDLAND *for March and April, 1896, and met with the approval of those whose opinion and judgment deserve the highest consideration. It is believed that this sketch forms the most complete and symmetrical single account of the life, public services, and personal characteristics of John J. Ingalls, that has yet been published; and it is, therefore, now reprinted and re-issued in more convenient shape.*

GRANVILLE H. MEIXELL.

*Midland College,
Atchison, Kansas,
April 15, 1896.*

CONTENTS

	PAGE
INTRODUCTION	9
HIS ANCESTRY	11
BIRTH AND EARLY LIFE	13
AT COLLEGE	14
AFTER GRADUATION	15
EMIGRATION WEST	16
EARLY POLITICAL CAREER	17
EARLY LITERARY EFFORTS	18
SUGGESTS GREAT SEAL	19
ELECTION TO THE SENATE	21
CAREER IN THE SENATE	22
HONORED BY HIS COLLEAGUES	24
SPEECHES IN THE SENATE	26
COMMAND OF LANGUAGE	27
ORATORICAL STYLE	28
LITERARY STYLE	30
"A STATESMAN WITHOUT A JOB"	33
WRITES FOR THE PRESS	34
HIS ESSAYS	35
AS A PLATFORM LECTURER	35
PERSONAL TRAITS	37
LITERARY TASTES	39
"OAK RIDGE"	39
CONCLUSION	41

" History is the essence of
innumerable Biographies."—CARLYLE.

JOHN J. INGALLS

A BIOGRAPHICAL SKETCH

———

GRANVILLE H. MEIXELL

JOHN J. INGALLS

JOHN J INGALLS
From his latest photograph by Kleckner, Atchison

JOHN J. INGALLS

A BIOGRAPHICAL SKETCH

INTRODUCTION

John J. Ingalls is, without doubt, the most distinguished statesman, the most brilliant orator, and the most fluent and versatile writer that the state of Kansas has ever produced. No citizen of Kansas has ever represented this commonwealth so ably in the deliberative councils and in the legislative forum of the Republic, or received such honorable recognition from his fellow-citizens in the state and in the nation, as has the man whose eventful life, distinguished public services, and peculiar personal characteristics, it

9

is the purpose of this essay briefly to trace and portray. While such a sketch must, however, of necessity be very condensed and incomplete, it is yet hoped that what little may be here presented from the mass of available material and authoritative data at hand, may be so carefully selected and so skillfully ordered as to form at once a review that is interesting and instructive, and an estimate which, however inadequate, may not be altogether unjust.

History, indeed, is largely composed of biography, and consists chiefly of a record of the achievements of great men, or of the movements and events in which great men were the foremost leaders and the principal actors; and the history of the past is revealed to us to a remarkable degree through the lives and deeds of the master-spirits who, consciously or unconsciously, have directed the trend of civilization into its modern channels, and have moulded and controlled, by their personal power and influence, the character and destiny of states and of nations. It has also been well said that "history is past politics; politics, present history." Examined from these points of view, a study of the lives and deeds of our prominent public men can not fail to prove highly interesting and truly profitable.

The professional and political career of John J. Ingalls is contemporaneous with the entire history of the state of Kansas, and is closely identified with the industrial development and the political vicissitudes of the same; while for over two decades, he has been one of the ablest, most popular, most unique, and most influential figures identified with the political affairs, the economic questions, and the social problems of the entire American nation.

HIS ANCESTRY

Ex-Senator Ingalls is the direct descendant of two noted Puritan families, coming on both his father's and his mother's side "from an unbroken strain of Puritan blood without any intermixture." His original ancestor on his father's side was Edmund Ingalls, who, with his brother Francis, came over from Yorkshire, England, in 1628, and founded the city of Lynn, Massachusetts. His father was Elias T. Ingalls, of Haverhill, Massachusetts, who was characterized as "a typical New Englander —aristocratic, austere, devout, scholarly —successful in business and respected by all." Mehitabel Ingalls, a first cousin of Elias T. Ingalls, was President Garfield's grandmother. On his mother's side, Mr. Ingalls is related to the noted Chase family, of which the late Chief-Justice, Salmon P. Chase, was a prominent member. The original member of this family was Aquila Chase, who came to America in 1630 and settled in New Hampshire. His mother, whose maiden name was Eliza Chase, is still living at

Haverhill, Massachusetts, at the advanced age of eighty-four years.

BIRTH AND EARLY LIFE

John James Ingalls was born at Middleton, Essex County, Massachusetts, December 29, 1833. He was the oldest of nine children, and is said to have been a "delicate child," "precocious in his intellectual development," and able to read intelligently when but two years old. At the same time, his "disposition was excessively sensitive, shy, and diffident," without giving any promise of the "virility and audacity" that have char·acterized his later career. He was educated in the public schools until he was sixteen, after which time he continued his studies preparatory for college under a private tutor. His literary genius had begun to manifest itself before he left the public schools, and his "earliest intellectual activity found expression in verse." When he was but fourteen years of age, he was "an occasional contributor to local and metropolitan newspapers, but always anonymously."

AT COLLEGE

He entered Williams College, at Williamstown, Massachusetts, in September, 1851, of which institution Dr. Mark Hopkins, at this time in the prime of his remarkable intellectual activity, was then President. Many of Mr. Ingalls' fellow-students at Williams "afterward achieved distinction and even prominence in political and other walks of life," the most famous of them being, no doubt, his distant kinsman, James A. Garfield, who was one year behind him in the collegiate course. After parting at college, the two friends did not meet again for eighteen years, when Mr. Ingalls was serving his first term in the Senate, and Garfield, who "had changed beyond recognition," "was a recognized leader and power in the House. Their old friendship, thus renewed, was warm and constant until Garfield's tragic death."

AFTER GRADUATION

After his graduation from college in 1855, Mr. Ingalls entered upon the study of law, and was admitted to the bar in his native county of Essex in 1857. The bold and fearless character of the states-man and the politician had begun to be foreshadowed in the college student, especially toward the close of his academic career. Into his graduating oration he incorporated views that were objectionable to the faculty, and which were cut out when the authorities revised his commencement production. When he came to deliver it, however, he spoke it as originally written, for which offense his diploma was withheld until 1864, after he had begun to make a name for himself in the West. Twenty years after granting him his first diploma, his *Alma Mater* honored him and itself by conferring upon him the degree of Doctor of Laws.

EMIGRATION WEST

Allured by a highly colored lithograph—a copy of which forms a much treasured ornament in a conspicuous place on the wall above the mantelpiece of his library—Mr. Ingalls emigrated to Kansas in the fall of 1858, and took up his abode at Sumner, a town founded by an enthusiastic adventurer from Massachusetts, John P. Wheeler by name, who had come to Kansas two or three years before this time. Sumner was located about three miles below Atchison, on the western bank of the Missouri river; was established as a rival free state settlement to Atchison, which was controlled by pro-slavery sympathizers; and at this time had a population of about two thousand, five hundred more than Atchison. Here Mr. Ingalls began to practice law, but

Sumner, being a "boom" town, had begun to decline before his arrival, and soon after became a veritable "deserted village," most of its population moving to Atchison, which had the advantage of a more favorable location, and had been built up by a more natural and substantial growth. In 1860, a tornado finally wrecked this ill-fated town, and Mr. Ingalls, though one of the last to desert it, also moved to Atchison and opened his law office in that town. He still has the official seal of Sumner in his possession; its motto reads, *Pro lege et grege.*

EARLY POLITICAL CAREER

Meanwhile, the future statesman had entered upon his political career, and was winning rapid promotion. In 1859, he served as a delegate to the Wyandotte Constitutional Convention. In 1860, he was Secretary of the Territorial Council. In 1861, he was Secretary of the State Senate. In 1862, he was elected a member of the State Senate from Atchison county. And changing his activities from the political to the military field, he served as Major, Lieutenant-Colonel, and Judge Advocate of Kansas Volunteers from 1863 to 1865. In 1862, and again in 1864, he also ran as a candidate for Lieutenant-Governor on what was then known as the "Union State Ticket," in revolt against the arrogant assumptions of such tyrannical political demagogues as "Jim" Lane and his followers, whose overthrow was not accomplished until 1866. For this course, Mr. Ingalls was accused of being disloyal to his party, but the circumstances seem to have made his attitude not only justifiable, but praiseworthy as well.

EARLY LITERARY EFFORTS

"For eight years after the war," writes J. W. D. Anderson, "Mr. Ingalls devoted himself to newspaper and general literary work—indeed, it was as a literary man that he first made a state reputation. We learned to know and admire the classical style, the incisive method, the wealth of words, and the fulness of information which have since made him so noted as an orator. Much of this literary work was in praise of Kansas, and as a genuine affection is nearly always returned in kind, Kansas soon came to love and to delight to do him honor." For three years he was editor of the Atchison *Champion*, "and subsequently won national reputation by a series of brilliant magazine articles upon themes of western life and adventure," the most noted of which were entitled "Catfish Aristocracy," "Bluegrass," "Regis Loisel," and "Cleveland, the Last of the Jayhawkers."

SUGGESTS GREAT SEAL

It is also of interest to note in this connection that Mr. Ingalls suggested the original design for the great seal of Kansas upon the admission of the state into the Union, together with the motto, *Ad astra per aspera* ("To the stars through difficulties"). Unfortunately, however, the simplicity and beauty of his original design were marred by the committee to whom it was submitted for adoption. The history of this emblematic device can best be given in ex-Senator Ingalls' own characteristic words:

"I was Secretary of the Kansas State Senate at its first session, after our admission in 1861. A joint committee was appointed to present a design for the great seal of the state, and I suggested a sketch embracing a single star rising from the clouds at the base of a field, with the constellation (representing the number of states then in the Union) above, accompanied by the motto, *Ad astra per aspera.*

"If you will examine the seal as it now exists, you will see that my idea was adopted, but in addition thereto, the committee incorporated a mountain scene, a river view, a herd of buffalo chased by Indians on horseback, a log cabin with a settler plowing in the foreground, together with a number of other incongruous, allegorical and metaphorical augmentations, which destroyed the beauty and simplicity of my design.

"The clouds at the base were intended to represent the perils and troubles of our territorial history; the star emerging therefrom, the new state; the constellation, like that on the flag, the Union, to which, after a stormy struggle, it had been admitted."

ELECTION TO THE SENATE

The first election of Mr. Ingalls to the National Senate, in 1873, came almost as a surprise to himself and his friends. Senator S. C. Pomeroy was a candidate for re-election, but he was suspected of dishonesty by some of the members of the State Legislature. His support, however, was so strong that there was no hope of defeating him, and the opposition in his party had not even united on a candidate. On the day that the houses met in joint session, State Senator York secured the floor, accused Senator

Pomeroy of bribery, exposed the fact that he had offered to himself (State Senator York) seven thousand dollars for his vote, and carried the money to the presiding officer's desk, requesting that it be used in prosecuting the offender. This sensation at once turned the tide away from Pomeroy, and Mr. Ingalls, who was in Topeka to argue a case before the Supreme Court, and who had received but one vote in caucus the day before, at once became a favorite candidate, and was elected upon the first ballot.

CAREER IN THE SENATE

Ex-Senator Ingalls' career in the upper chamber of Congress is so well known that it may be rapidly passed in review in this sketch. His record was so satisfactory to his constituents that he was returned to his seat in 1879, and again in 1885. In 1887, after the death of Vice President Hendricks, he was unanimously elected President *pro tempore* of the Senate, and this election was later, by a special rule which has since been followed, made permanent until the inauguration of a new Vice President; or until, in case the Vice President is living, the Senate should have changed its political complexion. While Senator Ingalls, therefore, was President of the Senate, he enjoyed all the honor, dignity, and distinction pertaining to the office of Vice President, and his family was accorded all the social precedence and recognition belonging to this position.

His public utterances upon the floor of the Senate were invariably marked by strong partisan bias, and his political opponents were frequently made to wince under his caustic and penetrating criticism and his flood of withering sarcasm; but yet his speeches were, at the same time, always characterized by a certain distinctive individuality and independence that marked the quality of their style and thought as being peculiarly his own. When, however, he was elevated to the office of Acting Vice President, he at once rose to the full measure and dignity of the high position to which his fellow-Senators had chosen him ; and as President of the Senate, he performed the functions of that office with unusual grace and with absolute impartiality.

The defeat of the famous "Force Bill," which Speaker Reed had pushed with characteristic dispatch through the House, was attributed by many of his party colleagues to Senator Ingalls. When he was requested to lend his aid as presiding officer to force the bill through the Senate, he "peremptorily refused to play this role," and sharply rebuked those who were attempting to resort to tactics not in keeping with the dignity of the Senate.

HONORED BY HIS COLLEAGUES

As a mark of their high respect and

of their appreciation of his uniformly "calm, impartial, and judicial" attitude as their presiding officer, the Senators, upon his retirement as President of the Senate, presented him with the clock that had counted time for the Senate from 1852 to 1890, which memento now adorns the wall above the landing of the stairway in the spacious hall of the Ex-Senator's residence; while upon the wall of his library, artistically engrossed and appropriately framed, is found the original copy of the following resolution, upon which comment would be superfluous:

"RESOLVED, That the thanks of the Senate are due, and are hereby tendered, to Hon. John J. Ingalls, a Senator from the State of Kansas, for the eminently courteous, dignified, able, and absolutely impartial manner in which he has presided over the deliberations and performed the duties of President *pro tempore* of the Senate.

Attest: ANSON G. McCOOK,
                            Secretary."

SPEECHES IN THE SENATE

Mr. Ingalls first won national fame as an orator while serving in the Senate, and many of his forensic efforts upon the floor of that body will never be forgotten. Whenever it was announced that the eloquent Senator from Kansas was to make a speech, the galleries and corridors of the Senate chamber were always crowded, and those who were so fortunate as to hear him, never came in vain. His speeches on "The Race Problem" and "The Financial Question," his eulogies on Senator Hill of Georgia and on Congressman Burnes of Missouri, and his debates with Senators Voorhees and Blackburn, are among his best known oratorical efforts in the Senate.

Concerning his well known reply to Senator Voorhees, it is worthy of mention that ex-Senator Ingalls regards it as 'the least creditable of all his performances, though it is undoubtedly the best remembered of all his public utterances; and he regrets that the occasion made such a speech in the Senate necessary.' He also claims that his criticisms of McClellan and Hancock had reference, not to their military records, but to their political attitudes, and that his remarks were perverted by his political opponents for the purpose of placing him "into a very disagreeable position."

COMMAND OF LANGUAGE

His command of language is remarkable, and his sparkling wealth of words seems to come to him as easily and as naturally as the poverty of language is a prevailing characteristic of most of his fellow-beings. He is equally fluent in conversation, upon the platform, or with his pen. A prominent newspaper correspondent, in reporting a recent interview with him, bears the following testimony to his wonderful conversational powers :

" Mr. Ingalls' language is so exact, his words balance his meaning so nicely, that the average conversational sloven-- and very few are not slovens in conversation—listen to the Kansas statesman, first with surprise, then with gratification, and finally with a strong ambition to emulate his niceties of speech. I defy any man of average conversational capacity to hold a thirty minutes' conversation with Mr. Ingalls without finding new powers of expression at the command of his own tongue."

ORATORICAL STYLE

As a public speaker, however, Mr. Ingalls' powers of expression seem to have attained their greatest range and their highest development. He is, moreover, a scholar, a philosophical thinker, and a close student of our social and political problems, as well as an orator and rhetorician. Many of his oratorical productions, viewed in the light of their magnificent and forcible style, as also with reference to their thought content, may, indeed, be termed "classical." A characteristic passage, taken from the introduction to his eulogy on Congressman Burnes, is here inserted for the sake of illustration :

"In the democracy of the dead all men at last are equal. There is neither rank nor station nor prerogative in the republic of the grave. At this fatal threshold the philosopher ceases to be wise, and the song of the poet is silent. Dives relinquishes his millions, and Lazarus his rags. The poor man is as rich as the richest, and the rich man is as poor as the pauper. The creditor loses his usury, and the debtor is acquitted of his obligation. There the proud man surrenders his dignities, the politician his honors, the worldling his pleasures ; the invalid needs no physician, and the laborer rests from unrequited toil. Here at last is Nature's final decree in equity. The wrongs of time are redressed, injustice is expiated, the irony of fate is refuted, the unequal distribution of wealth, honor, capacity, pleasure, and opportunity, which makes life so cruel and inexplicable a tragedy, ceases in the realm of death. The strongest there has no supremacy, and the weakest needs no defense. The mightiest captain succumbs to the invincible adversary who disarms alike the victor and the vanquished."

In a similar compact, epigrammatic style, is his oft-quoted estimate of Lincoln :

"Abraham Lincoln, the greatest [leader] of all, had the humblest origin and the scantiest scholarship. Yet he surpassed all orators in eloquence, all diplomatists in wisdom, all statesmen in foresight, and the most ambitious in fame."

LITERARY STYLE

The limits of this essay will permit the insertion of but two specimens from his more purely literary productions not composed for public delivery — one in poetry and one in prose — and both written since his retirement to private life. The first is a sonnet entitled "Opportunity," the original draft of which was written on the back of an envelope in traveling on a train from Kansas to

Washington, and which appeared in fac simile manuscript form in the New York *Truth*, in February, 1891. The arrangement of the lines here given follows the original copy of the poem :

OPPORTUNITY.

" Master of human destinies am I!
    Fame, love and fortune on my footsteps wait.
    Cities and fields I walk: I penetrate
Deserts and seas remote, and passing by
    Hovel and mart and palace, soon or late
    I knock unbidden once at every gate!
If sleeping, wake; if feasting, rise before
    I turn away. It is the hour of fate,
    And they who follow me reach every state
    Mortals desire, and conquer every foe
Save death; but those who doubt or hesitate,
    Condemned to failure, penury and woe,
Seek me in vain and uselessly implore.
I answer not, and I return no more!"

As a good specimen of his prose literary style, the following paragraph, contributed in 1893 to a symposium by our leading literary men and women on "How to be Happy," is here inserted :

" Happiness is an endowment and not an acquisition. It depends more upon temperament and disposition than environment. It is a state or condition of mind, and not a commodity to be bought or sold in the market. A beggar may be happier in his rags than a king in his purple. Poverty is no more incompatible with happiness than wealth, and the inquiry how to be happy, though poor, implies a want of understanding of the conditions upon which happiness depends. Dives was not happy because he was a millionaire, nor Lazarus wretched because he was a pauper. There is a quality in the soul of man that is superior to circumstances, and that defies calamity and misfortune. The man who is unhappy when he is poor would be unhappy if he were rich, and he who is happy in a palace in Paris would be happy in a dug-out on the frontier of Dakota.

"There are as many unhappy rich men as there are unhappy poor men. Every heart knows its own bitterness and its own joy. Not that wealth and what it brings is not desirable —books, travel, leisure, comfort, the best food and raiment, agreeable companionship— but all these do not necessarily bring happiness, and may co-exist with the deepest wretchedness; while adversity and penury, exile and privation, are not incompatible with the loftiest exultations of the soul.

'More true joy Marcellus exiled feels,
Than Cæsar with a Senate at his heels.'"

"A STATESMAN WITHOUT A JOB"

When Senator Ingalls fell a victim to the Populist upheaval in Kansas in 1891, and was obliged, much to the regret of the country at large, to yield his seat in the Senate to Mr. Peffer, his political adversaries took delight to refer to him by his self-applied title of "a statesman without a job." In this respect, however, their expectations were not realized, for the man of genius and industry is never out of employment. They failed to recognize that a statesman must not necessarily hold public office in order to be either successfully or advantageously employed, and that if his services as a public man have been of consequence, men will not likely let his talents remain unemployed as a private citizen. Upon his retirement from public life, Mr. Ingalls had a number of exceedingly tempting offers — both in the East and in the West — to accept the editorship of prominent newspapers, all of which he declined, mainly because their acceptance would require him to transfer his family and his citizenship out of his adopted state.

WRITES FOR THE PRESS

After his return from a trip to Europe, his library, his pen, and the lecture platform, have profitably occupied his time and talents, and a number of timely articles upon the principal economic, political, and social questions of the period, have appeared from his pen in the leading periodicals of the country. Among his more practical articles, may be named those on "The East and the West," "Politics and Newspapers," "Immigration," "Politics," "The Social Malady," "Capital and Labor," and "Our Political Parties;" among his more purely literary essays, those on "Oratory," "Blaine," "The Tragedy of '81" (Garfield), and "The White City" deserve special mention.

HIS ESSAYS

His essays are always in great demand, are said to "command larger prices than those of any other man in America, with the exception of Oliver Wendell Holmes and James Russell Lowell," and are not only intensely interesting, but highly instructive as well. They do not express ideas merely struck off at random, but embody the valuable results and conclusions of years of faithful study and ripe experience. It is a real misfortune that these writings are not extant in collected form, and that they are only accessible in the files of the papers and magazines in which they were first published, or in clippings from the same.

AS A PLATFORM LECTURER

Mr. Ingalls has also been in great demand as a popular platform lecturer since retiring from the Senate, his services in this capacity command the very highest prices, and as a lecturer and orator he has probably only two peers on the American platform—Depew and Watterson. This field of activity opened to him spontaneously, unsought by himself, and contrary to the usual experience of the successful orator, it is, strange to say, absolutely distasteful to him. In a recent interview he expressed himself as follows on this subject, and his own words are quoted here because they help to reveal one of the characteristics of the man :

"I have a dread of public speaking. When I approach the place where I am to make a speech or deliver a lecture, I am filled with a nameless terror. Sometimes it becomes almost uncontrollable, and I am tempted to turn and fly. For more then twenty years, at the bar, on the stump, on the platform, and in the Senate, I have practiced the art, but the trepidation is as great now as when I began. But for this drawback, I should enjoy lecturing, because it brings one in contact with the best people of many communities ; and my engagements are so arranged that the traveling is not arduous.''

Mr. Ingalls' platform lectures are not cast into any stereotyped form, are always related to our current political and social problems, and as he is a student of all affairs of public interest, and "of the changing times," he gives to his lectures "a contemporary flavor from day to day through his knowledge of current public affairs." The subjects of his principal lectures are "Plutocracy and Anarchy," "Dives and Lazarus," "Political and Social Problems of Our Second Century," and "Garfield." It is worthy of mention in this connection that ex-Senator Ingalls never permits tickets to be sold, or gate money to be taken, for any speeches that he delivers in Kansas. This rule he violated but once, and then permitted himself to do so, not for his own profit, but to help to raise funds to clear a charitable institution from debt.

PERSONAL TRAITS

The tastes of a man are always a good

index to his character. The clothes he wears, the company he keeps, and the books he reads and ponders—these declare the man. Mr. Ingalls is tall and striking in his personal appearance; dignified and self-possessed, yet withal friendly and polite, in his demeanor; and while affecting some peculiarities of dress, always dresses tastefully and well. While he would not permit any one to make free with him in the sense in which some men suppose good fellow-ship must be cultivated, he is yet approachable by the humblest laborer as easily as by the most exalted in rank, position, and influence. He is neither the "aristocrat" that he is sometimes represented to be, nor yet the "agriculturist" in the sense in which he is represented to be such. He personally superintends the care of his lawns and orchards, but he does not engage in "farming." He enjoys exercise in the open air, and horseback riding is his favorite physical recreation.

"OAK RIDGE"

Residence of John J. Ingalls

LITERARY TASTES

Ex-Senator Ingalls' literary tastes are of the highest classical order, and his reading is confined almost entirely to the standard authors in English and American literature. The Book of Job, Shakespeare — especially "Hamlet," Gray's "Elegy," Shelley's "Skylark," Keat's "Eve of St. Agnes," Longfellow's Poems, Hawthorne's "Scarlet Letter," Dickens' "Pickwick Papers," and Drummond's "Natural Law in the Spiritual World" — these, with others by the same authors, and by other standard authors of the same class, form his favorite reading; and the continued reading and study of such literature doubtless, in a measure, accounts for his varied vocabulary, his own fine literary style, and for his pure literary tastes.

"OAK RIDGE"

"Oak Ridge," located on a slightly wooded elevation overlooking the city of

Atchison from the southwest, is the name given to Mr. Ingalls' beautiful and cultured home. His former home, located on the bluffs of the Missouri river, was destroyed by fire, and with it most of his valuable library and unpublished manuscripts, while he was living with his family at Washington. He bought "Oak Ridge" upon his return to Kansas, and here, removed somewhat from the commercial turmoil of the city, he enjoys with his family one of the most refined and most comfortable homes in Atchison. He is the father of eleven children, seven of whom — three sons and four daughters — are still living. Mrs. Ingalls, to whom the Senator has always been a hero, has been to him a most loyal wife and helpful companion, and is, moreover, a most faithful and devoted mother to her family, and an ideal housekeeper in the management of her home and in the education and control of her children. By the salutory

power and influence that Mrs. Ingalls is
so constantly exerting over her family,
the domestic side of Senator Ingalls'
home, in spite of his long career in
public life, has not suffered in the least.
His home is a cheerful and happy one,
in which the higher literary and artistic
tastes, and the nobler ideals of life, are
assiduously cultivated, and in which the
bond of affection is sincere and strong.

CONCLUSION

The historian of contemporaneous
events, or the biographer of men still
living, can record facts and events, and
he may even express his individual opinion of their character, their relations,
and their importance, but he can do little more than this. The principal service that he can perform—and it is im-
portant that he should always perform
this faithfully and well—is to gather the
material which the future historian and
biographer must have in order to enable

them to write the final account, and to formulate the final estimate, of men, events, and movements, after long years have elapsed, after the passions and prejudices of the present have passed away, and after unerring time has sifted what is fundamental and enduring from that which is merely adventitious and transitory. This final account will be written some time ; and, whether sooner or later, whenever it is written, it will be approximately true and just.

The contemporary chronicler must, therefore, be sure to make his record as complete and accurate as possible, and he has rendered his best service to posterity when that has been accomplished. How much of what he has gleaned will be gathered into the final repository, how much will be discarded, what will be the relative value of what is pre-served, and how much will ultimately be added thereto, the future alone can definitely make known.

This should not, however, in the least discourage the historian or the biographer from making a close, intelligent, and unprejudiced study of the leaders of his day—whether he adopts all their opinions, and accepts all their conclusions, or not—and also of the various events and tendencies of his own time. The historian of the past has furnished him with the data which he must have to enable him to form his own estimate, and thus help to form the final estimate, of the history of the past ; and since the historic chain has never been broken, and never will be, he can go on linking event to event, cause to effect, and consequent to antecedent, and so may even in his own day, to some extent, estimate the influence of contemporaneous actors and events upon their own period, and may also approximate their probable effect upon the development of the future.

The study of human life and destiny,

whether in the concrete or in the abstract, in the individual or in collective society, is always of the highest interest and importance; and the more it is pursued without bias or prejudice, the more profitable the results will be for ourselves, and the more valuable for posterity.

In such a philosophic spirit of historic inquiry, this biographical sketch has been written; and however great its inaccuracies and short-comings may be, the study would not prove entirely in vain, even though no one but the writer himself should derive any benefit from the effort. Such efforts, however, are at no time in vain, if the motives that incite to them are honest and right; nor can a life so full of varied effort and exalted activity as John J. Ingalls' eventful and distinguished career has been, fail to leave its lasting impress upon the age and the nation in which he lives, or to be a powerful factor and influence in giving direction to the life and character, and in shaping the destiny and welfare of the American people in the future.

The final history of the latter half of the nineteenth century, and the final estimate of the character and achievements of the leading public men of this period, will not be written during the life-time of the present generation, and they may not be written until a number of generations shall have passed away; but whenever the final account shall have been formulated, and whenever the final estimate of the most distinguished statesmen and foremost leaders of this epoch shall have been made, the name and fame of John J. Ingalls will occupy a unique and conspicuous place among the list of illustrious Americans of this eventful age who loved their country most and served her interests best.